WALT DISNEY'S

WINNIE the POOH
And A Day For EEYORE

BOOK CLUB EDITION

One summer day, Winnie-the-Pooh was walking down the road that went to the old wooden bridge. The bridge was one of his favorite places. He liked to stand on it and look down at the river slipping slowly by.

As Pooh walked
under the pine trees,
something bounced
on his head.

"My goodness!"
cried Pooh. "It's a fir-
cone. And a very
good one, too!"

Pooh was looking at his perfect fir-cone
and didn't see the big root sticking up from
the path. *Ooops!* Pooh tripped over the root
and went tumbling down the hill.

Pooh landed right in the middle of his favorite bridge.

"Where did my fir-cone go?" Pooh said, looking up the hill. "Oh, bother! It's rolling right into the river!"

Pooh watched the fir-cone plop into the water and float away.

Then Pooh noticed
something very
strange.
"That's funny! My
fir-cone fell in the
water on that side of
the bridge and came
out on this side! I
wonder if I can do
that again!"

Pooh gathered more fir-cones and some sticks and went back to the bridge. He stood on one side of the bridge and threw everything into the river. Then he ran to the other side of the bridge.

"There's one, and another, and another— they've all come through! And the sticks are even faster than the fir-cones!" said Pooh. "I can't wait to tell everyone!"

"Piglet! Rabbit! Roo! I've got a new game to play. It's called 'Pooh Sticks.' I named it after myself," Pooh explained. "I can't tell you about it, but I can show you."

So they all went down to the river.

"Now everyone gather some sticks," Pooh said. "When we throw them off this side of the bridge we run to the other side and see who wins!

"Are you ready?" Pooh asked. "Throw!"

Then Piglet, Pooh, Rabbit and Roo all ran to the other side of the bridge.

"Here comes mine!" cried Roo.

But it wasn't a Pooh Stick at all. It was
Eeyore floating in the river!

"Dear me, Eeyore," called Rabbit. "Are
you waiting for somebody to help you out of
the river?"

"That would be nice!" Eeyore answered,
bobbing up and down.

"What shall we do?"
asked Piglet.
Then Pooh said,
"I've got an idea! If
we throw a big rock
next to Eeyore, the
waves will wash
him to shore!"
Everyone except
Eeyore thought it
was a fine idea.

Pooh got a big rock and lifted it up to the rail of the bridge. He aimed at a spot near Eeyore, and gave a big push. *Splash!* The rock fell very close to Eeyore. In fact, it fell *on* him.

"Look! There he is!" said Rabbit, pointing down the river. And there was Eeyore, climbing out of the river onto the shore. Pooh's idea had worked...sort of!

They all ran over to the dripping donkey.
"How did you fall in?" Rabbit asked.
"I was bounced in," Eeyore said gloomily.
"I expect Tigger bounced him!"
whispered Piglet.

Just then, out of the woods bounced Tigger.

"Tigger, did you bounce Eeyore into the river?" Rabbit asked.

"I didn't bounce him," Tigger said. "I was behind him and I coughed!"

"Bouncing or coughing, it's all the same," Eeyore said.

But everyone knew that Tigger had bounced Eeyore into the river.

"You really should think of others before you go bouncing about!" Rabbit said to Tigger.

But Eeyore shook his head. "Why should Tigger think of *me*!" he said. "Nobody else does!" With his head hanging low, Eeyore walked away.

"Eeyore seems gloomier than usual today. Does anyone know why?" asked Pooh.

"No, Pooh," Rabbit said, "but you're right—I've never seen Eeyore so gloomy!"

"Well then," Pooh said, "I'll just follow him and find out what's wrong.

"What's the matter, Eeyore?" asked Pooh, after he caught up with the little donkey. "You seem so sad."

"Sad? Why should I be sad?" Eeyore answered. "It's my birthday. The happiest day of the year!"

So that was it! thought Pooh. It's Eeyore's
birthday and no one remembered!
"Wait right here!" Pooh yelled to Eeyore.

Pooh hurried home
as fast as he could.
On the way, he met
Piglet.

"It's Eeyore's birthday and I'm going to
give him a jar of honey!" Pooh said.

"And I shall give him a red balloon!"
Piglet said, and he ran home to get it.

Pooh found a very fine jar of honey in his cupboard. He started back to Eeyore's house. He hadn't gone very far when a funny, rumbly feeling began to creep over him.

It told him that it was time for a Little Something. Very soon, the honey jar was empty and Pooh's tummy was full.

"Oh, bother!" cried Pooh. "I've eaten Eeyore's birthday present! Now all I have to give him is an empty pot!"

Then Pooh had an idea.

"I shall go see my friend Owl!"

Pooh went to Owl's tree house. He asked
Owl to write "Happy Birthday" on the
empty pot, and Owl did.

"What a splendid idea," said Owl. "An
empty pot can be a very useful present."

HIPY PAPY BTHUTHD
THUTHDA
BTHUTHDY

Meanwhile, Piglet was running through the woods with a big red balloon.

"Eeyore will be so pleased with this balloon! He won't be gloomy anymore, and…"
Kaboom!

"Oh, dear!" Piglet said, holding up what was left of his big, red balloon. "I've hit a branch with my balloon, and now I haven't got a balloon at all!"

Piglet found Eeyore by the river.
"I've brought you a present, Eeyore!" he said. "It was a beautiful, big, red balloon, before it popped…"

Eeyore stared at the broken balloon.

Just at that moment,
Pooh arrived with his
empty honey pot.
"I've brought you a
birthday present,
Eeyore!" said Pooh.

"It's a very useful pot," Pooh pointed out, "and it's got 'Happy Birthday' written on it."

Eeyore examined the empty pot.

"It's for putting things in," Pooh explained.

Eeyore picked up the broken balloon and put it in the pot. Then he took it out and put it in again.

"Gosh, you didn't have to get me anything," said Eeyore, smiling, "but I'm very glad you did!"

HIPY PAPY BTHU
THU HDA
BTHUTHDY

"And I'm very glad that I thought of giving you a useful pot to put things in!" Pooh said.

"And I'm very glad I thought of giving you something to put in a useful pot!" Piglet added.

"Now we have another surprise, Eeyore!" said Pooh. "Come with us!"

So Eeyore, Pooh and Piglet set out for the bridge.

Just as they got to the top of the hill, there were shouts of "Surprise!" and "Happy Birthday!"

Eeyore looked down and saw all his friends wearing party hats.

Of course, "Eeyore's friends" didn't include Tigger. Tigger hadn't been invited to the party because he had been thoughtless and bounced Eeyore into the river. But just as they began to eat Eeyore's birthday cake, Tigger bounced in.

"You've got a lot of nerve showing up after what you did to Eeyore!" Rabbit said, watching Tigger gobble up a big bite of cake.

"I think Tigger should leave!" Rabbit said sternly.

"Awww, let him stay!" Roo pleaded.

"What do you think, Christopher Robin?" Pooh said.

Christopher Robin
thought for a moment.
"I think..."

Everyone waited to
hear Christopher
Robin's answer.

"I think we all ought to play Pooh Sticks!" he said.

"Pooh Sticks?" Tigger said happily. "Oh, boy! That's what Tiggers do best!"

So they gathered on the old wooden bridge and played the game for many happy hours. And Eeyore, who had never played Pooh Sticks before, won more times than anybody else!

But poor Tigger didn't win at all.

"Tiggers don't like Pooh Sticks!" he said grumpily.

"Congratulations, Eeyore! It's been a delightful party!" Owl said, and he flew off toward his tree house.

Then Eeyore noticed Tigger walking away
sadly.

"Tigger!" Eeyore called. "I'd be happy to tell
you my secret for winning at Pooh Sticks!"

"You would?" Tigger answered, suddenly
looking his old, cheerful self.

And off they went together.

Pooh and Piglet and Christopher Robin
watched them walk away.

"Tigger is all right, really," Piglet said.

"Of course he is!" Christopher Robin agreed.

Pooh thought for a minute. Then he said,
"Everybody is all right, really. That's what I
think. I don't suppose I'm right."
But he was.

NICE FOR PIKNIC

RABBITS HOWSE   PIGLET

KANGAS HOUSE

SANDY PIT WHERE ROO PLAYS

POOH BEARS HOWSE →

WHERE THE WOOZLE WASNT

FLOODY PLACE